בס"ד

This book belongs to:

לד' הארץ ומלואה

Please read it to me!

Dedicated to our dear grandchildren
Shlomo Yechezkel, Rachel Aliza, Ester Bryna, Shoshana Bayla, Yisrael Leib,
Menucha Chaya, Shira Bracha, Leeba Ahuva and Tehilla Bracha Ita

May they always shine with the Light of Torah
And May Hashem shower them with all His blessings.

Marion and Benjamin Tuchman

When the World Was Quiet

First Edition - Shevat 5764 / January 2004

This book is dedicated to my grandson, Akiva Chaim Friedman. Phyllis Nutkis

This book is dedicated to my parents, who always encouraged and supported my artwork, and to Robert Deibler, who always liked a good story. Patti Argoff

Editor: D.L. Rosenfeld

ISBN: 1-929628-14-5
LCCN: 2003109750

HACHAI PUBLISHING
Brooklyn, New York
Tel 718-633-0100 Fax 718-633-0103
www.hachai.com   info@hachai.com

Printed in China

Glossary:

Hashem - G-d
Torah - the Five Books of Moses;
the law and wisdom contained
in the Jewish Scripture and Oral Tradition.

When the World Was Quiet

by Phyllis Nutkis
illustrated by Patti Argoff

Adapted from the Midrash
(Sh'mos Rabah, 29:9)

Hachai
PUBLISHING

When Hashem gave us the Torah,
the whole world was quiet.

The people did not talk.

The babies did not cry.

The birds did not chirp.

The fish did not splash.

The geese did not honk,

and the ducks did not quack.

The sheep did not "baaa."

The goats did not "maaa."

The chickens did not cluck,

and the roosters did not crow.

The turkeys did not gobble.

The cows did not moo.

The wind did not swish.

The leaves did not rustle,

and the ocean did not crash.

There was no sound except for Hashem's voice.

He said, "I am the One and Only Hashem."

And then...

...in His quiet, quiet world...

...Hashem gave us the Torah, because He loves us.